WEAVING WORDS

An anthology of short stories and poetry by Neston Writers

Maureen Allsop	Margaret Croft	Ishbel Faraday
Debbie Furr	Pauline Hignett	Jean Maskell
Sheila Phelan	Chris Ryan	Linden Sweeney
Beth Taylor	Mary White	Jenny Williams

Pumpkin Press

Copyright © 2025 Neston Writers. All rights reserved.

The characters and events portrayed in this book are fictitious. Any similarity to real persons, living or dead, is coincidental and not intended by the author.

No part of this book may be reproduced, or stored in a retrieval system, or transmitted in any form or by any means, electronic, mechanical, photocopying, recording, or otherwise, without express written permission of the author or publisher.

ISBN: 9798305968637

Cover design by: Lydia Croft

CONTENTS

About Neston Writers	3
Maureen Allsop	4
Margaret Croft	10
Ishbel Faraday	26
Debbie Furr	35
Pauline Hignett	40
Jean Maskell	50
Sheila Phelan	58
Chris Ryan	61
Linden Sweeney	71
Beth Taylor	80
Mary White	87
Jenny Williams	95
Acknowledgements	100

ABOUT NESTON WRITERS

The origins of our group took place during a summer break from a creative writing short course we all attended in 2019. Unwilling to pause for a number of weeks we began to meet at our local community centre where we still meet once a fortnight to this day.

We continued our creative efforts via zoom during lockdown thanks to Linden, our leader and friend.

Our membership has grown in recent times and it has been a real pleasure to widen our writing circle. We take turns to set topics or themes to inspire us and produce a wide variety of interpretations either in prose or poetry. We have also brought in other writers to support and further our talents.

We enjoy meeting for social events and always seem to have plenty to chat about, often becoming quite noisy and always laughing.

In deciding to produce our anthology we have all been surprised by how much work we have amassed and enjoyed revisiting our poems and prose.

We hope you enjoy our selection as much as we have enjoyed belonging to such a friendly and generous group.

MAUREEN ALLSOP
Little Neston

A little bit of silliness is how I would describe my first four pieces. The last is dedicated to Roy.

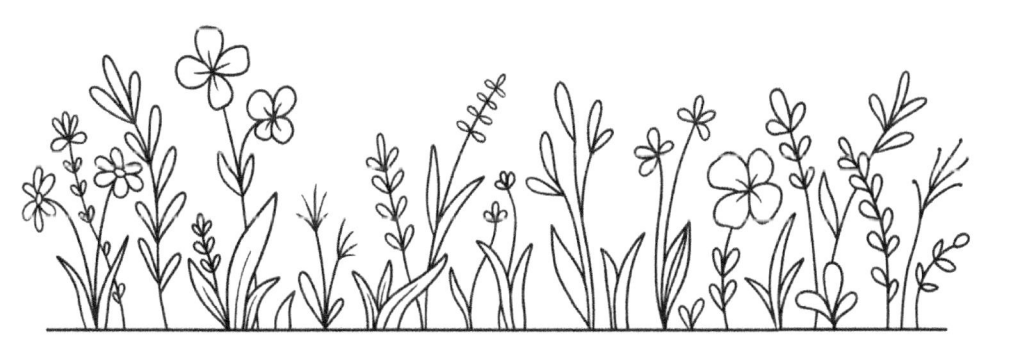

THE MOON

The man in the moon looks down on me
His gaze is intent, so what does he see?
The happy me laughing and bright
Or the sad me – howling, crying, sighing all night.
Sometimes I'm grumpy, cross as can be
No one it appears can agree with me.
But when I'm in love and at the moon I stare
I know my love sees it, and together we share
The very same moon, though we're miles apart
And both of us feel each other's strong beating heart.

I now watch the moon beside my little grandchild
Where have the years gone when like her I was quite wild,
Seeing funny moon faces and a cow leaping high
Up, up and over that huge moon in the sky.
The cat and the fiddle witnessed that jump
The camel though didn't, and he got the hump.
But the owl and the pussy cat they too had great fun
As they sailed in the light of the moon, not the sun,

So my thanks to the mysterious man on the moon
Yes, the one that saw the dish run away with the spoon!
We know you'll watch over us 'till the day that we die
That's why we are never lonely with you in the sky
And not afraid in the darkness because your bright silvery light
Bathes the earth's blackness so no evil's in sight
And now my old friend it's time for goodbyes
As the dawn breaks forth and you fade from our eyes.

THINGS I DID AS A CHILD

Roly polys down grassy slopes
Carefree children, full of hopes.
Climbing trees, fishing in streams
Days were such fun, nights full of dreams.

We loved to play hopscotch, skipping as well -
And picking daisies down in the dell.
Blind man's bluff plus hide and seek,
I cheated quite often, couldn't resist a peek.

A little bit older, and quite a lot bolder -
We played sardines, jammed shoulder to shoulder!
Kiss chase came next – I ran oh so slow
The sweet embraces that followed left me aglow.

I then was a bride, my prince at my side
My family, my all - my joy and my pride.
The years have flown by, I'm no longer wild
But deep, deep inside me lives that carefree young child.

WHAT AM I

I'm round and fat with a hard inside
And the wind will blow me far and wide.
I'll come to rest on Mother Earth,
Close by the tree that gave me birth.

With my own little cup I come complete,
But I'll never have any hands or feet.
I used to live up very high
And watch the clouds race in the sky.

The squirrels will come and bury me deep
And during the Winter I'll peacefully sleep,
Until spring arrives and I begin to stir
And changes with me start to occur.

An Acorn

CATS

Cats may sit on a mat,
Or maybe curl up in a hat.
We often stretch out on a bed,
Once we've been suitably fed.

We love to lie in the sun
Or chase away pigeons for fun.
We'll poop in someones front garden,
Never saying 'I do beg your pardon'.

We'll allow ourselves to be petted -
Once you've been carefully vetted.
And often stay out overnight
Just to give our humans a fright.

We'll turn up our noses at dinner,
Last week's favourite no longer a winner.
Our humans give in to our whim
And new food fills our bowl to the brim.

So, as a cat I must have the last laugh,
Dogs have Masters, cats have............staff!

WHERE HAVE YOU GONE

Where have you gone, are you hiding from me?
I've searched high and low, but I still cannot see.
But you must be here
I can feel you near.

Ah, I see you now and my heart beats like mad
I'm happy again, not sorrowful and sad.
I love you so
Please don't go.

Let's sit and talk, we're together once more
I've so longed for this moment, it's you I adore.
You again hold my hand
In make-believe land.

A mist descends through which I cannot gaze
And now I'm running, running as though lost in a maze.
I start to cry
Is this goodbye.

I glimpse you again but you're so far away
Can't breathe and I panic – stay, stay, oh please stay.
I love you so much
I yearn for your touch.

As I slowly awaken, my cheeks wet with tears
I'm starting to realise my very worst fears.
It was a dream
I silently scream.

for Roy, from Maureen

MARGARET CROFT
Liverpool

Although I had always enjoyed writing creatively, I seldom made time for it. This changed however, when I became part of a group of friends who share this interest and meet regularly - something which has definitely increased my productivity! It has also provided plenty of inspiration, in the form of the prompts we take turns to supply for each meeting. Of course, whether the subject matter comes from a topic suggestion or a sudden random thought, the outcome is the same. These are a few of my own favourite pieces (both fiction and poetry) based on ideas from either source.

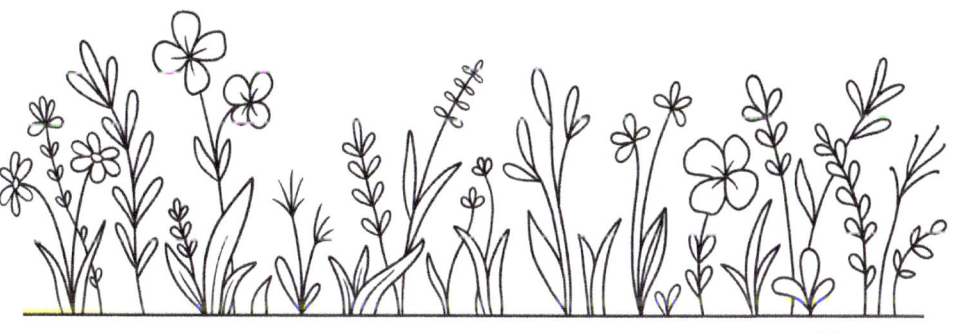

THE MAN IN SEAT 61

'It was such a challenging play, but you really need to see it – you would love it!' enthused Sarah, sipping her chai latte.

'Well, I'm certainly keen on anything that raises awareness about climate change, but...' Lucy hesitated, 'I'm not comfortable about going to the theatre alone.'

'You'll be fine, I often do it. We singles still have a right to enjoy ourselves, don't we? And it's the sort of place where loads of people go on their own. You never know, you may even meet someone.' Sarah grinned cheekily, then added 'Anyway, we're not bothered about that, are we? Plus, the Prince Regent is a really interesting venue. It was an old music hall, very ornate with lots of gold filigree and so on. It's been closed for ages and has only just reopened.'

'Really, why?'

'Some sort of health and safety thing, balcony rail too low or unstable or something. Apparently, there was an accident a number of years ago – someone from the front row of the balcony ended up in the stalls. Anyway, the whole interior was completely reconfigured after that, using crowdfunding. Now it concentrates on the work of aspiring young playwrights, and edgy dramas. Right up your street!'

'Mmm... I think I will go after all,' smiled Lucy, 'especially as you say it's only a tenner to get in. You never know, I might meet an aspiring young playwright!'

*   *   *

It was raining hard when Lucy joined the shuffling queue outside the theatre, the steady downpour splashing from her hood onto her face, smudging her mascara and turning her protruding curls into rats' tails.

'Let's hope we get in soon,' said a voice behind her. 'I've heard it's a really good play and can't wait to see it. It's by a new young writer - her first big break: something I'm hoping for myself, one day.'

Lucy spun around to see a tall, fair-haired young man with sparkling blue eyes. She couldn't believe her luck, this sort of thing never normally happened to her. Then, with embarrassment, she realised how bedraggled she must look and wondered whether this really was a chat up line, or just polite conversation. But he smiled at her and continued to talk in a friendly, relaxed manner. He asked where she was sitting.

'I'm in the front stalls, but I don't know whether I'll have a very good view of the stage. I'm in row D, seat 60 – which I think might be right at the end of the row.'

'Yes, there's only 64 seats in a row so not the best view! But hey, guess what, I'm in row D, seat 61!'

This really couldn't be happening she thought, it was too good to be true! Lucy settled down to watch the play, occasionally stealing sly glances across at the guy next to her – and feeling little flutters in her stomach. As the drama unfolded however, Lucy became increasingly absorbed in the play, which was sombre and comic in turns.

'Can I buy you an interval drink?' he asked as the curtain fell at the end of the first act.

'Oh yes please – I just need to nip to the ladies' first. See you in the bar.'

Lucy was anxious to sort out her hair and fix her make up before facing the bright lights of the theatre bar. Unfortunately, there was a long queue and so it was quite some time before she emerged and made her way to the cocktail lounge. But he was nowhere to be seen. She completed two careful circuits of the room, before deciding that maybe she was in the wrong place and set off towards the circle to see if there was another bar. There wasn't.

The final call for the audience to return to their seats sounded whilst she was still upstairs. Lucy hastened back down towards the stalls, but the second half had already commenced as she returned to the auditorium and searched for her seat in the semi-darkness. Not wanting to cause a disturbance, she walked down the far aisle, looking for her seat near the end of the row. She counted four rows back from the front – this must be row

D. But something was wrong. Her companion had not returned to seat 61, and in fact the people seated on the other side of her seemed to have spread out along the row, leaving only one seat at the end. Lucy sat quietly in seat 64 and tried to immerse herself in the second half of the play. She found it hard to concentrate; questions spinning round in her head. Where had he gone? Was he angry that she had taken so long and stormed off? Or maybe he'd changed his mind about her when he saw her in the full glare of the interval lights? Or was it something she'd said? But surely none of those things would have resulted in him leaving the theatre altogether?

    Eventually the play ended and everyone rose to their feet in enthusiastic applause; Lucy participating half-heartedly, her mind still on the mystery man who was no longer in seat 61. Final bows taken, the cast left the stage and the lights came back on. As the people around her scrabbled for coats and bags, Lucy scanned the audience. Maybe he'd decided to sit elsewhere, in order to avoid her? She couldn't see him and, disappointed, returned her gaze to her own seat. She stiffened, hairs rising on the back of her neck. Her seat number was clear to see - seat 60, the last in the row. There was no seat 61.

    She somehow stumbled back out into the foyer, her legs barely supporting her. But she couldn't bring herself to leave with the rest of the audience, who were now spilling out of the exit into the dark, wet street where she had queued only a couple of hours before. Noticing a man starting to clear up any debris carelessly left lying around, she approached him, her voice quivering as she spoke.

'Excuse me, I'm a bit confused… I was at the end of the row in the stalls, but my seat number was 60. I thought there were 64 seats in each row?'

'Yeah, there used to be,' he drawled. 'But the whole place was refurbished after that young writer chap was killed some years ago. He fell from the balcony during the interval, landing on one of the seats at the far end of the front stalls. Anyhow, the new seats are bigger and more comfortable now - and only 60 in each row.'

A FRIEND IN NEED

Sammy lay shivering in the darkness. His mother had read him a story about elves and goblins before, kissing him goodnight, she'd turned off the light and gone downstairs. He wasn't shivering because he was cold, his bed was warm and snug. Nor was he shivering because he was afraid of the dark - even though his toy cupboard and wardrobe loomed like great black buttresses in the darkened room. Sometimes he was afraid someone - or *something* - might be hiding in there, ready to pounce. But tonight his fears were rather more prosaic, but equally scary. His fear even had a name: Bertie Rogers.

Sammy had looked forward to starting 'proper school', and had indeed enjoyed his first weeks there and settled in well. But then he had accidentally bumped into Bertie, whilst running around in the playground. The collision had taken Bertie off guard and he had fallen over, grazing both his knees, and the unbidden tears had hurt Bertie's pride even more.

Now, Bertie was in the year above, and considered himself a tough guy, like the action heroes he loved. He was big for his age, and looked up to by many in his form; and was usually accompanied by a group of devotees, the inner ring of his circle of admirers. And now Sammy had inadvertently made sworn enemies of them all - his stuttered apologies having fallen on deaf ears.

That night, Sammy tossed and turned, before falling into fitful sleep, haunted by confused dreams, combining the events in the playground with the goblins from his bedtime story. It was barely light when he awoke, and the rest of the family were still slumbering. He stumbled to the bathroom in semi darkness. Standing on his stool to wash his hands, he peered into the mirror to see his own pale face reflected back at him.

But as he went to look away, the face changed. It was no longer his own wan reflection, but a cheerful, rosy cheeked image with twinkling brown eyes, surprisingly wearing a pointy green hat, which matched his strange, bright green frilly shirt. Sammy realised he must still be half asleep, and that this strange apparition must simply be the last vestiges of a dream. He shoved his knuckles against his eyes and rubbed hard, blinked and looked again. The peculiar face was still there - and now it started speaking!

'Hello Sammy, good to see you,' it said, in a high-pitched, squeaky voice. 'I know you've been scared but I'm here to help.'

'Who, who… er… *what…* are you?' Sammy stammered.

'My name is Pippin and I'm a pixie.'

'But you can't be real, and I don't see *how* you can help me deal with Bertie. You're not even very big.'

'Oh, but I am real - and I can be lots of sizes. Usually I'm very tiny, but that can be very useful at times. I can even hide in your school bag and come to class with you. I can be invisible when I want, so your teacher won't see me- nor will Bertie! My job title is 'Friend in Need' and so I'm only here when you really need me, like now.'

Sammy stared at him, open-mouthed. 'I, I must be dreaming,' he muttered, but the pixie just grinned at him, then started to fade, so that once again it was just Sammy's own reflection in the mirror.

When he returned to bed, Sammy fell into a deep sleep and was nearly late for school. When he got there, he noticed a commotion in the playground. Bertie's grandmother had bought him a new action hero figure, which he'd smuggled into school, in defiance of the parental rule that expensive toys remain at home. But while he was hiding behind the annexe, showing it off to friends, a group of older boys had come to see what the fuss was about.

'Oh cool!' cried one, 'I've asked for this one for my birthday - can I hold it?'

Feeling simultaneously proud and a bit scared, Bertie had relinquished the toy, hoping the bigger boy would not run off with it.

All would have been well, but more boys arrived, and one tried to snatch it, resulting in a tussle. It was at this point, as Sammy arrived, that the bell rang, and the teacher called for the classes to line up. The two big boys immediately let go of the action figure and, as

Bertie watched in dismay, it fell into the grid under the annexe drainpipe. Unfortunately, the grid had been broken the previous day and was awaiting repair, so the toy vanished through the hole and into the slimy darkness below.

Bertie tried to put in his hand to retrieve it before the teacher noticed, but his fist was too large and anyway he couldn't have reached far enough down.

'Oh no, it's lost - and my mum will be mad at me!' he wailed. 'Can anyone help? Please, oh please help me!'

'Here's our chance!' said a squeaky voice from Sammy's jacket pocket, as he stood there, staring. 'Move fast - tell Bertie you've got small hands and can get it back for him. Off you go!'

Sammy walked across the playground in a dream, and nervously made the offer to a tearful Bertie. Sammy's small fist fitted through the hole, but his arm wasn't nearly long enough to reach the toy. Suddenly though, the plastic figure seemed to rise up to meet him.

'Here, grab it quick, it's heavy for me to hold,' puffed Pippin from inside the grid.

Sammy closed his fingers around it, and carefully drew it out, as he felt the little pixie jump back into his pocket.

'Sammy, you're a marvel! I don't know how you did it: you must have special powers just like my action heroes!' Bertie enthused. 'Friends?'

Sammy smiled and nodded happily, unperturbed by his teacher's rebuke for being late to join the line, which was already processing into the building.

When he got home from school, Sammy hunted in his bag and pockets for his tiny friend, but he was nowhere to be seen. Instead, a business card had been left in his jacket, which simply read:

Friend in Need pixie services - there when you need us most.

Sammy gazed at his own smiling reflection in the bathroom mirror as he cleaned his teeth that evening, before snuggling into his bed for a really good night's sleep.

THE WEAVER'S SHED

A master craftsman, he works with silent intensity.
With patient deliberation, he ensures the pattern is repeated
Exactly, at every turn.
He is a perfectionist.

He did not falter in his task
When I entered.
Maybe he didn't notice me?
I'm glad not to have disturbed him.

His long dark limbs suggest
He might be happier working outdoors.
But all his wiry strength and concentration
Is on the task in hand.
And, anyway, such delicate work
Needs shelter.

It's a poor old ramshackle place,
In which to express his artistic soul.
A hostage ray of sunlight
That carelessly slipped through a crack in the wood,
Illuminates specks of dust in the still air:
 Dancing in the golden glow.
Like ballerinas!
But he pays them no heed.

He must be getting hungry now -
Working so hard for so long
Look - the pattern is almost complete.
It will soon be time for a break.

Our companionable silence
Is broken by the suggestion of a sound:
A soft buzzing, like a tiny saw.
I feel annoyed -
Might this interloper destroy his art?

My companion sits and watches,
Motionless and phlegmatic.
The web is complete,
And dinner has arrived.

HOT WATER

Hot water has a smell
All of its own.
Not salty like seawater,
Or fresh with the memory of countless summers,
Like rainwater.
Just a sharp, clean smell
All of it's own.

Bath water has a sound
All of its own.
A running, rushing sound
Of pouring water
Frothing scented bubbles.
Or the slow plink plink
Of the last drips,
Disturbing the plangent gleam
Of the placid lake
Beneath the shining taps.

But I like best
The plashing, sploshing sound
Of water when I bathe,
With rubber ducks for company.
(Sounds from below
Muffled and contorted
Like a distant land).
Cleansing my mind from the accumulated grime
Of convoluted thoughts,
Each splash and dribble
Transports me back through decades:

A child again.
And, as usual…
…in hot water!

BLACK ICE

'Mum!' shouted Jack excitedly, 'it's snowing!'

His mother gazed out at the barely visible flakes. Jack was always first to notice things - his bright eyes discerning what others couldn't see. Sometimes it was a blessing - he'd later observed black ice on the path ahead and his mum avoided a tumble. More often it was simply irritating. Teachers, annoyed at disruption to lessons, usually dismissed his remarks. Even as an adult he was often ignored - such as when, travelling to America, he'd pointed out an iceberg to a crew member on the Titanic.

ISHBEL FARADAY
Frodsham

The first four pieces of work reflect my interest in using different poetic forms. The fifth is simply a short fictional story of the type I enjoy writing.

BIRTHING A POEM

This poem may never reach you,
never find its promised destination.
Its embryonic form may fail to grow
enough to grace the page or fill the auditorium.

This poem may never make it
into print – who then will see
each stanza length, each punctuation mark,
the neat enjambment linking line to line?

This poem may never speak
its verse aloud – who then will hear
each word's intended stress, each pregnant pause,
the sound of patterns dancing in the air?

And if this maelstrom
of ideas were harnessed – who knows which ones
would blossom into words – who knows
which words would be discarded and which chosen?

This poem may never reach you

PORT APPIN

How calm the cows that roam the shore,
how succulent the grass,
how quizzical the look they give
to cars that sometimes pass
between the grassland and the sea
along the wayward track
which takes them on to reach the pier
and brings them rumbling back.

How straight the lonely heron stands,
how still the morning loch,
how undulant the ebbing tide
exposing ancient rock
where seaweed lies and limpets cling,
where thrift grows wild and free,
the places that I loved are now
but memories to me

THE SCULPTOR

In 1932 Ben Nicholson and I visited the Rumanian sculptor Constantin Brancusi in his Paris studio……I encountered the miraculous feeling of eternity mixed with beloved stone and stone dust……the simplicity and dignity of the artist; the inspiration of the dedicated workshop.
— Barbara Hepworth, *Writings and Conversations*
pages 61-2

He holds the chisel, familiar to his touch,
carves essence of bird from virgin stone.
From workshop windows open to the sky
angled light illuminates each cut.

His feet, inch deep in stone dust as he works,
imprint a circle round the sculptured form.
His purpose is perfection, his hands' caress
will cause the earthbound shape to soar and fly.

Unfettered by wing or feather it will rise,
a weightless, upward thrust of grace,
at one with all things made it will become
a spontaneous, living joy.

A GAME OF CAT AND MOUSE

This is the tale of Martha the mouse
who lived, safe and secure, in her little mouse house,
nothing could touch her, not even the cat
who, everyday, patiently, watchfully, sat
eyeing the mouse hole expectantly for
movements of Martha approaching the door.
She would come to the entrance and poke her head through,
saying, 'You can't come near me, I'm not scared of you.
In my little mouse house I'm as safe as can be,
try all you like, you can never catch me.'
Time passed as time does and the cat became older,
Martha the mouse grew bolder and bolder.
She saw that his legs were arthritic and slow
and his eyesight was failing, so bravely she'd go
right out of the mouse house, a few steps away
from the danger that no longer seemed so and say,
(as mice who are teasingly confident do)
'You can't come near me, I'm not scared of you.
Even out of my house I'm as safe as can be,
try all you like, you can never catch me'.
When the cat was asleep she would do as she pleased,
come out of the mouse house for titbits of cheese,
and when she was feeling especially brave
she would climb on his back and give him a wave
as he opened his eyes and stretched out his toes,
for it's blatantly obvious, everyone knows,
a cat who is old doesn't pose any threat
to a mouse who is younger and fitter and yet,
danger was looming in the shape of a cat

not arthritic, slow, short-sighted, or fat,
but sprightly, clear-eyed, energetic and thin,
recently purchased and newly brought in
to add to the household, the perfect addition
to empty the house of the mouse population.
So when Martha decided to next venture out,
to nibble some cheese and to saunter about,
she wasn't prepared for the pending disaster,
she could run fast but the new cat ran faster.
Martha's demise was quite painless and quick,
a pounce and a grab of the tail did the trick.
Today you might hear, as you pass her mouse house,
the faintest of whispers from Martha the mouse,
ghostly and wistful and always on cue,
'You can't come near me, I'm not scared of you.
In my little mouse house I'm as safe as can be,
try all you like, you can never catch me'

A GRAND DAY OUT

I was ironing when I heard the 'plop' of the post on the door mat. Tucked between junk mail and the monthly bank statement was an envelope that caught my attention. This was no ordinary envelope – its cream, embossed paper displayed a unique postmark with the royal crest and the iconic words *Buckingham Palace* Inside was an invitation card:

> *The Lord Chamberlain is*
> *commanded by her Majesty to invite*
> *Dr and Mrs John Medway*
> *to a Garden Party*
> *at Buckingham Palace*
> *on Wednesday 29th June 2022 from 4 – 6 pm*

    I was still in shock when John came home from work. Apparently he had known for a while that his name had been put forward and he wanted to surprise me. I spent the next few weeks preoccupied with practising my curtsey and deciding what to wear, (easy for him – just hire a morning suit). In the end I plumped for a blue, flowered day dress, a wide brimmed hat in the same delicate blue, higher heeled shoes than I would normally wear and a white clutch bag, (a style favoured by Kate so I can't go wrong there!).

    *   *   *

We took a taxi, (ridiculous price), from our hotel to the palace, were ushered beneath the famous balcony, across the inner courtyard and through a side entrance onto the lawn. The brass band struck up *God save the Queen*, only it wasn't the Queen who appeared on the steps. She was unfortunately indisposed that day. We had to make do with Charles and Camilla, (disappointment number 1).

We quickly discovered that the formation of greeting lines requires a certain level of jostling skill, (which we hadn't practised). The couples either side of us obviously had and were much more adept at it than we were. We soon found we had forfeited our prime position, (disappointment number 2), quickly followed by disappointment number 3. I might, at least, have had a chance to talk to Charles about my new, organic, raised vegetable beds but he was fast disappearing to the line opposite while Camilla was moving in determined fashion towards ours. Her pink ensemble was complemented by a long, tightly furled umbrella, (an item we would soon wish we had thought to include).

I was in half-curtsey mode when she swept past without so much as a glance, (disappointment number 4). This was just before the heavens opened. Within minutes I was literally rooted to the spot, my high heels sinking slowly into the ground, rain dripping off the brim of my hat, dress clinging to my legs. With some difficulty on my part we made it to the refreshment tent. It really shouldn't have been but it became the highlight of the day. Between us we consumed two of the 27,000 cups of tea dispensed that afternoon, six of the 20,000 sandwiches, (cucumber with fresh mint and black pepper were my favourite), and eight of the 20,000 cakes, (they were minute to be fair).

I've just finished compiling a small photo album – my personal reminder of the day. (I've erased the disappointments from my mind. The rain is a distant memory. The shoes have gone to Oxfam.) The first photo is of the two of us looking smart and elegant with the palace in the background. I managed to capture Camilla too, before she walked past us and there's a distant one of Charles, his back towards us, chatting to people on the opposite side.

But the one I like best is of the tables in the refreshment tent, laden with the tiniest sandwiches and cakes, each one a small, delicious mouthful. In the pocket at the back I've put our monogrammed napkins – evidence, if any is needed, of *a grand day out*.

DEBBIE FURR
Neston

I moved from Kent to Neston in 2019 and was persuaded to join my friend's Walking group which led to me joining an Art Group which led to me joining this Creative Writing Group. How fantastic is that!

THE RED DOOR

She remembered it like yesterday, 20 years had passed, but even now it remained very real.

The terror of the night started early around 5pm, she could still smell Mum's cooking, Shepherds Pie, her favourite.

She noticed the shadow on the wall, it had a human shape she thought, but that was just her imagination she said to herself, she was after all a very sensible 9 year old, it was probably from the street light , when the shadow moved she jumped and then it disappeared, weird.

Mum called for dinner yummy as always. 'Your turn to clear the table Susan,' Mum said after dinner was finished

Susan started to clear the table trying very hard not to drop anything before she saw the shadow again, it moved towards her and she dropped a plate and screamed

'MUM THERE'S SOMETHING IN THE KITCHEN,' she was terrified and could not move for fear of whatever it was.

Mum came running into the kitchen 'What on earth's the matter?' she said.

'THAT,' said Susan pointing at the wall.

Mum was exasperated 'What? There is nothing there!'

Susan looked, whatever it was had gone. She finally got ready for bed, her sister was already in bed reading a book.

'You alright?' said her sister.

'Fine,' said Susan and climbed into bed.

She was fast asleep when she was woken by something holding her head, she was terrified and could not move while this Alien hand slowly crawled down her face, it stopped at her chin, then she saw the arm, body and those awful fluorescent blue eyes. The scream would not come. It stuck in her throat. Her sister woke and boy could she scream. Whatever it was let go of her and vanished.

Mum came rushing in at the sound of Susan's sister still screaming.

They left the house that same week, and nothing would possess Susan to ever go into the house with The Red Door ever again.

THE SADNESS

She watched the children, they were having so much fun in the garden.
Doreen called to them 'Michael, brush the mud off your trousers.'

Michael gave a loud moan 'But mum we are having fun.'

'Michael,' said Doreen loudly.

'Ok,' replied Michael sulkily as he stood and brushed the mud off then carried on playing.

Doreen carried on sitting by the window watching the children's antics, it made her happy, so she thought!

Sandra, her daughter, came in the room with two mugs of tea on a tray, Doreen preferred a cup and saucer but she knew Sandra preferred a mug,.

Sandra heard Doreen talking .

'Who are you talking to mum?'

Sandra put down the tray and looked at her mother quizzically, 'The children in the garden darling they are having such fun.'

Doreen carried on watching, and Sandra smiled sadly at her mother with a tear in her eye.

'Back in a minute mum, just getting some biscuits!'

.   Sandra walked to the kitchen, the nurse saw her tears. Georgina was a lovely nurse, when she spoke it was with kindness and stoicism.

'It's ok Sandra, you can say it, dementia sucks.'

THE MOON

The mirror saw it first and kept still in anticipation, the rest of the room hummed with excitement, it was always the same when the day occurred.

Everything had been polished by the mistress of the house, she was so proud of the house and on this day especially everything was shining like new, before the event.

In the forest outside the animals and birds were asleep already, save one, he was preparing for the event as well. He walked silently through the forest, his magnificent mane glistening in the light of the

setting sun, his eyes shone an emerald green, would this be the day, would it he thought, it had been so long.

He came to an opening in the forest and saw the hill above the house. He walked slowly up it - don't rush, be calm. The sun had gone down and it was dark, it was nearly time.

Slowly the white orb rose in the dark sky and shone down on him, he howled like the wolf he was in anticipation. He started to glow and shine, his mane became golden and his eyes a beautiful amber, he became the man again after so long.

He saw the door to the house open as he walked down the hill, the house shone brightly in the moonlight, even the furniture was happy. The mistress was at the door, his hair was now white it had been so long, but finally the master was home.

PAULINE HIGNETT
Neston

Writing can be a solitary occupation. It is a privilege to share my work with our group and receive encouragement from them. I continue to learn so much from the other writers both from their supportive comments and their own poems and prose.

ROMEO AND JULIET

I watch them as they progress down the road,
each secure with a hand to hold.
Both in anoraks: sensible coats,
with scarves secured around their throats.
They are chatting away, unaware
that I am comforted as I stare.
To think that time has made them whole
the two are one in synchronised stroll.
They move quite slowly, age dictates,
their time together defined by fate.
She steadies him: he anchors her,
a matching set, a couple, a pair.
I wonder as they amble in their fashion,
if they've ever felt the throes of passion;
or caused each other careless pain
nothing ever quite the same again?
Of their late night conversations,
their hopes, their dreams and life's celebrations.
Do they view their past now as a blurred romance
through the twostep, the quick step, or a different dance?
Whatever life has thrown their way
they are steadfast companions before me today.
My hope for them is simply this,
that they end their days with a tender kiss.

LIFE THROUGH A LENS

Photographs give us memories we hardly knew we had,
moments skimmed from life, subjects viewed as good or bad.
Our infant selves preoccupied with long abandoned toys,
embarrassing clothes, lacy frocks for bonny baby boys.
Pretty dresses smocked with carefully embroidered stitches,
Halloween, fancy dress a row of smiling but mischievous witches.
A photograph of two people tells the story of three: one hidden.
The invisible snapper demanding a smile, 'say cheese' when bidden.
Birthday parties with presents from long forgotten classmates.
Christmas holidays, celebrations, pictures marking each important date.
We see ourselves as others see us, greet relatives we've never met.
Outmoded clothes in black and white, where an unchanging scene is set.
A snapshot, unheard conversations, decades brought to light.
Their past revealed to our present sealed now, forever in plain sight.

Thoughts, ideas and memories frozen, shuttered, fixed in time.
Ghosts in a monochrome world, posed in an organised line.

Writing on the back, 'Aunty Jean Ainsdale Beach 1954'
A small insight, a rare day out, suggesting so much more.
Albums carefully organised their failing sticky photo corners slipped
Places long forgotten, meaningless scenes, father's face, tight lipped.
Memories otherwise dissolved through the passage of time
In the essence of the moment, preserved they are mine.
Photographs give us memories we hardly knew we had
Moments skimmed from life, subjects viewed as good or bad.

A FLAMBOYANCE OF FLAMINGOS

I'm Fenella a fabulous flamingo, pink to the tips of my wings.
I stand on one leg in the water just doing my elegant thing.
I'm in the pink today, a flamboyance of fantastic feathers,
always looking glorious in the fairest or foulest of weathers.
One day I'll dance a fandango which fortunate people will flock to see,
I'll be fantastic, feminine, fancy and famous.
They'll all want to flatter me, I will of course love the fuss,
and flaunt my fantastic self, enjoying the fanfare and rightful flurry.
But my leg is beginning to ache, I'll swap soon so not to worry.

I'm Francis the forlorn flamingo, finding no reason for fun
my neck is tired of bending just to feed my new born son.
I have to put my head upside down scoop up the chosen shrimp
I've done it so much in this lagoon I'm feeling both jaded and limp.
I'm five feet tall, it's a long way to stretch my sinuous neck
and now I must wade to find a new supply, something tasty to peck.

But in a while I'll stand on one leg and hide myself amongst the rest.
Perhaps one day I'll fly far away but for now it's me and that busy nest.

I'm Fiona the fussy flamingo a flippant nickname from friends,
I like to fly to a fancy place just north close to lake's end.
Here I can fondly look at my reflection, finesse my feathers if flat,
Feed carefully. I can't be fat my self-esteem doesn't allow that.
But most of all, I like to show my best to the cameras each day,
I flounce and flaunt with a flourish, a feast of fashion they say.

TINY PIECE OF THE PAST

It felt important for some inexplicable reason to clean the now empty house. She knew it made no logical sense, but felt duty bound to make sure the property developer didn't think badly of her. Some deeply ingrained sense of pride or perhaps a last chance to peel back the final layer of her years happily sheltered by this old building.

So, there she was already exhausted from 'the move', on her hands and knees cleaning the floor. Then wedged under the skirting board she saw the tiny piece of card and knew straight away it would have a letter F emblazoned on it.

She rocked back on her heels and looked at the jigsaw piece and smiled at the memory. How could something so small and insignificant hold the key to unlocking so much emotion?

The picture came into her head like the repeat of a TV drama.

'It's supposed to be the f....ing Flying Scotsman,' he bellowed.

'What have you done with it?' he accused.

There followed much more of the same while the hoover bag was emptied the carpet was lifted and the whole house sent into a state of uproar.

*   *   *

For days afterwards he wandered around the house muttering and grumbling. If she was honest their relationship hadn't been 'on track' for a while and this tantrum only served to emphasise the situation. Following a hunch and craving peace she decided to check all his pockets in case the devious piece of card had made a last bid for freedom.

What she did find, however, was an absolute cliché and clear evidence that without his precious letter F he was just a 'Lying Scotsman' after all. So, jigsaw notwithstanding, he rapidly became her permanent missing piece.

SURPRISE DISCOVERY

It's the end of a long sunny day at the seaside. I am stranded on Bournemouth Station with four sandy, sticky and tired small boys waiting for our train. There is an unavoidable delay. We've succeeded in finding a seat we can all sit on, played 'I Spy', had an overpriced and much argued over ice cream and I've now resorted to 'The Alphabet game'. For each letter, always excluding x, they must take it in turns to name a part of the body. A dangerous category I know but I'm desperate. I don't know anyone in Bournemouth should the words become too explicit. We've reached the letter B and as I hear 'bum' and 'boobs' I turn away from the squirming mass of arms and legs giggles and snorts of children delighting in their own audacity.

    As I relax, I become aware of the photo' booth opposite our seat. The curtain is drawn and all I can see is a pair of very still feet. The owner of the feet is clearly female as I can also see a small area of drab green pleated skirt. Even though it is so hot our mystery lady is wearing stockings which are wrinkled around her ankles. Her chosen footwear sandals, reminding me strongly of my Grandma's. They are beige with a brogue like pattern stamped into the leather. An old fashioned brown handbag has been placed on the floor. Time passes. Nothing changes. I begin to catastrophise; to think in headlines: 'Bournemouth Body in Booth' or 'Photo Fatality'.

    The boys have reached G and are still occupied in an unseemly manner, so I stroll self consciously towards the booth. Still no movement. I look around asking myself, 'is this my responsibility? What shall I do? I've never seen a dead body and the boys!' I gather my courage and tentatively ask in a truly British way, 'Excuse me. Are you alright in there?'

'No,' comes the tremulous reply.

Such a relief, now I may only be required to call an ambulance. I cautiously draw back the curtain to reveal a very hot and distressed lady who in fact looks like my Grandma. I smile encouragingly, and she tearfully explains that she has followed all the instructions and is sitting very still waiting for her photographs to appear. She is afraid to move in case they are still being developed, but it has been half an hour since the flash bulb flashed.

How do I avoid making her feel foolish? There is however no choice as I am audibly alerted that the letter P is imminent. I quickly retrieve the photos' from their designated slot outside the booth. I hand them to her waxing lyrical about how good they are, suggesting she treats herself to a cup of tea.

I swiftly turn to witness four small boys holding a body part beginning with P and the guard blows the whistle!

JEAN MASKELL
Raby Mere

Our group retains the best elements of a writing group and we learn, inspire and encourage each other as supportive friends. This work represents a cross-section of my interests - Ireland, women's experiences and industrial heritage. At The Crossroads *was written just before the demolition of the Salford and the Birkenhead gasometers.* Crossing To Ireland *is my reflection as a dual British/Irish citizen of having two places that are home.* The Launch *is a tribute to the town of my birth, Birkenhead and the shipyard men who built the Mauretania 2, launched in 1938.* A Heartbeat in the Snow *was inspired by a WW1 photo taken in 1917 of a soldier playing with a kitten in France.*

AT THE CROSSROADS

The slow breathing lung of the town inhaled, rose and fell so slowly, that no-one really noticed. Unaware of the gas pushing through veins of pipes under their feet, through meters, tripped by slots of pennies - to mantles, back-kitchen ovens; to boilers and fires and yellow spluttering street-lamps; to warm and light, and sometimes kill.

When full, the great tanks cast dark shadows, blotted out the sun. But in summer, like a sleeping giant, the tank descended into the earth and lovers taking shelter behind the gasworks wall in the moonlight could see the stars.

Then still, as years pass. She has breathed her last sigh, weeds around her feet, but still soars above the town with grace. A monumental memorial to life and strife in a northern town. A fragile beauty, a cathedral of steel lace, whose edges of rust are dazzled away by the glint of diamond-white search-lights as a cloud drifts across the sun. There is order in her symmetry, a geometry of community, connected, many angles in the web, yet held together, standing tall. The Stonehenge of Salford, empty, yet full of mystery and wonder.

Here at the cross-roads, lay lines of the past, whisper in the breeze

'Take me to the gas-yard wall and kiss me one more time, like before'

…before the traffic roars from the city, through the brownfield plains. The terraced streets are gone. Smart investments, apartments, will rise, for digital workers, where riviters and dockers once walked to work; where women in headscarves carried shopping bags home from the Co-op; where children in balaclavas pushed prams of coke through the grey slush of winter. The pattern is broken, crushed.

    The demolition man drops his cigarette butt and watches it fall. It's a long way down. Time to get to work.

CROSSING TO IRELAND

Mid-sea, the rhythm
beating heart of the boat
measures, calms time,
as I lean on the rail,
no land in sight.

Tossed cotton balls of cloud
drift across forget-me-not sky,
casting cerulean shadows
across the vastness
of grey sea.

Flashes of sunlight illuminate
virescent depths;
a mystery of random photons,
reflecting the surface,
yet passing through.

How is it possible
to be in two places
at one time,
live two lives?
Forces pull both ways.

Behind, a chaotic wake
of motion, copper-stained streaks,
drizzle away
in a train of white lace
across the Irish sea.
Here is Peace.

Between the lands - no choices.
Carried in a waiting dream
of calm sea
neither leaving nor arriving.

Storms are long forgotten
in the cycle of years unbroken.
Salt-air gulls
ride the current;
holding; forward, forward.

Underwater lightning, linking
Celtic roots. Cambrian and Wicklow,
Pennine and Mourne rivulets
meld in the breathing sea.
Rise in crested waves.

Then the shock of land
Familiar hills form and rise
through mist on the horizon.
My heart quickens, welcomes,
the embrace of home.

THE LAUNCH

Thirty thousand tons of steel.
Welded, hammered, forged
with men's lives
thunders into the sea.

Angled to hit the water and dip,
'Hold your breath lads!'
She rights, and cuts through
the river like a knife.

Turning on the tide
to face the sea
that will carry her aloft
to foreign lands, adventure.

She knows no fear
of storms yet to come.
For the bride of the sea,
the journey has just begun.

LOVE LOST

The shards of heart
the shattered sharp
prisms within
the mirror
the image
that was us
in pieces
scattered
in places hidden
places
not safe to walk
where only the moon
touches memory
where no one
sees a glancing
silver glint
cut
dark night
reflect that life
that light
that
once
was love

A HEARTBEAT IN THE SNOW

Nothing was said, the night the guns ceased.
Boys, aged with ash rimmed eyes, slumped,
waited for the next, but none came.
Only the soft whisper of snow falling on no man's land.

Curious glances, echo headed voices.
Is that a moan? A groan of the wind?
Is it the child we passed on the road,
dead in its dead mother's arms?

While my own son, warm in his cradle,
so far away...
No. No. Do not think of him today.
Draw down the blinds of my mind and turn away, away.

A bayonet raised to skewer a rat, pauses.
Two eyes, wide with terror, flash in the light.
The bony sack of damp fur, draws blood
as tiny kitten claws cling fast to my hand.

Crying for help, for fear, and food, till,
our scraps devoured, with the little fellow
curled in the crook of my arm,
we slept.

And when I woke, I swear he smiled that Cheshire cat smile
and stretched, pushing tiny paws against the khaki.
And then the tears came,
when I remembered it was Christmas Day.

SHEILA PHELAN
Galway

I am honoured to be made a visiting member of your group. I find the work I hear there talented and inspiring; a big thank you to all. I live in Galway (visiting family in the beautiful Wirral area as often as possible) and am part of two writing groups; Creative Writing with Geraldine Mills (poet) and a casual Writing Club of stalwarts similar to your own group. Ship in a storm is an acrostic based on memory, a painting I saw in a Turner exhibition in The National Gallery in Dublin and the second is Galway based.

SHIP IN A STORM

Shuddering heave and groan of oak pounded with
mountain peak waves,
Hammering roars of tide, wind and swell,
Invade each pore, drown the senses and
Plough on relentlessly.

Into the depths the bodies fall with
No escape.

Alone the ship will flounder on some rocky reef.

Still someone clings to jagged beams
Timbers that float
On a churning cauldron. 'Merciful Lord' a desperate
plea
'Rescue
Me.'

(Inspired by William Turner painting A Ship against the
Mew Stone *c.1814.)*

SKY HIGH 5AM OVER GALWAY

I awake hearing the sky distant rumble
Thirty thousand feet over Galway.
A jet speeds with arrow intent to the far away.
My head pillowed in bed softness
I think of the life inside.
Coughs, body movements, white noise,
seated, packed, folded in carton fashion
passengers hurtle huddle above cotton cloud.
They sleep, dream, worry, anticipate
their lives on a forward eternal trajectory.
A voice, pilot professional may say,
'We are now cruising at thirty- five thousand feet
over the west coast of Ireland, hope to land in
'predictive' hours,
speed 500 miles per hour.'
Some listen intently,
others aware only of an intrusion in thought or
subconscious.
I think of what always seems a miracle in a sardine tin,
400 tons suspended in velocity and time.
Swift drop, belly lift down to earth
where I close a sleepy eye and drift away.

CHRIS RYAN
Chester

Whilst choosing the poetry and flash fiction I wanted to include in our anthology I realised I was drawn to my writings done during Covid restrictions. At this time, living alone, I had time to reflect and reminisce and so produced writing relating to my feelings and observations of life at this strange time. Although we could not be together as a group we were able to communicate through Zoom meetings set up by Linden, our inspirational and efficient friend.

MOMENTS OF WONDER

The song is shrill delivered with force
Clear notes repeated with one final burst
Loudly they call to each other.
I stop and listen to their call
A ripple now a chattering fall
Then up with a flourish.

There will be two; tiny and skulking,
Hidden in the leaves, watching and waiting.
Will they ever appear for me?
Do they sing for joy or just to show
Courage and bravery even though
Their territory is secured?

I search the branches scanning both ways,
One comes into view, I see the cocked tail.
My smile comes, this bird I know.
But now in flight, fast, direct, quickly,
Its short wings whirring energetically
Caught in the light for only a moment.
I follow the movements, eyes squinting,
Hold my breath and then sigh; fleeting
Moments of wonder; now gone.

IT HAPPENED JUST AS THE CLOCK STRUCK MIDNIGHT

The men in the queue shuffled their feet. Some looked at their watches, some flicked a glance at their phones. They didn't acknowledge each other, they didn't know each other but they were all here for the same reason.

He was not at the front of the queue. He hadn't thought that others would be as desperate as himself to even consider queuing like this, but he could see the front of the queue and he could see the door.

A few seconds passed, then the door opened. A masked and gowned person stepped out. A few of the men murmured, someone quietly started to cheer, then one person started to clap, another joined, then another. Now they were all clapping, stamping their feet, waving their phones, laughing, turning to each other.

He joined in. But then they all fell silent. They felt in their pockets and took out their masks. It was going to be alright. It wasn't scary at all. They still queued, they still didn't speak to each other. They would wait until it was their turn to step forward.

Although it was midnight - they would all have a haircut.

LET'S PRETEND

Let's pretend that we're on holiday
And this garden is our world
Look closely at what's growing
And appreciate each furl
Of bracken that has crept in
Amongst the bluebells and the white
And wonder at how nature works
In the warmth of May sunlight.

Let's pretend we're on a journey
Through years of planting and reflect
On the failures and successes
All surrounded by our hedge.
Some plants are in the right place
And can offer scent or shade
But many should be moved now
To enjoy the space we've made.

Let's pretend that we intended
To grow this rampant, wooded dell
Where hidden corners give us
A place to think and dwell
On the people we remember
Through the plants they gave to us
Over thirty years and longer
Each extra year a plus.

I'm pretending I am sitting
Here with you just by my side
Enjoying all the blues and greens

Other colours only mine.
Watching you as you relax
In the cool and leafy shade
Making my heart yearn
For more memories to be made.

This is our secret garden
Where still I wait for you
Despite already knowing
That you can never be here too.

ONE FRIDAY

Jacob was eight when he first saw Jesus die. He was holding his mother's hand tightly but he still felt alone and very small. There were people pressing all around him.

'Has Jesus really died?' he whispered and looked up at the people. One lady heard him, she whispered back,

'No, no of course not.'

Then his mother looked down and he could see tears in her eyes.

They had been in town for hours. Jacob had first seen Jesus near the Eastgate, he had been walking with a donkey. There was a lot of noise, people were cheering and waving. Then he had seen him on the Rows above the shops. He seemed to be at a party, he was eating and drinking. Jacob could see Jesus was not very happy, but he couldn't understand what he was saying.

Then his Mum had taken his hand and they had hurried past the Cathedral. Jacob saw three wooden crosses outside, he pulled at his Mum's hand but she didn't stop.

When Jacob saw Jesus again he was being pushed by the crowd. Some men pulled him up the Town Hall steps. He was wearing something on his head which looked like a crown but there were red marks on his face and he looked as if he was crying.

People were shouting, 'Crucify him, crucify him!'

Jacob looked at his mother, she was whispering, 'No, no.'

Then everyone went silent. That's when Jacob whispered, 'Has Jesus really died?

THE SLOW JOURNEY

Let me take you with me
To a place in Africa, in the east
We're on a slow, calm journey
Close your eyes and concentrate.
It's early morning as we set off
To miss the searing heat
We are going to spend time waiting,
Sitting, not on our feet.
But it will be worth it
As the sights that you will see
Will stay with you forever
As they have done for me.

The earth, rust-red and shimmering
Stretches before us endlessly
As we sit side by side just waiting
And watching silently.
In the distance an impala herd grazes
The young oblivious and free
Adults alert and aware always
Legs trembling, ready to leave.
Their ears prick up and heads turn
They sense a nearby threat
It isn't us but a predator stalks
They recognise the scent.

Sinuously the lioness moves
They are in her sight
We watch, they listen
Then all explode into flight.

No kill this time, we breathe again
It's not their turn nor ours
We are here to observe only
Protection is not in our power.
Only acacia trees stand out
To offer any shade
So we drive on observing
Any movement to be made.

Sat beneath an acacia we listen
Crackling twigs, now soft cries
And some movement in the grasses
Means our wait is satisfied.
At first only one small pup
Emerges fearfully to the left
Then a tumbling of animals
Coats, soft brown, like velvet.
It's a whole hyena family
Looking at us innocently
But their food has been scavenged
Death has been here recently.

Early morning is disappearing
And soon the animals will too
To find the shade for resting,
The hours are all too few.
We view giraffes in the distance
With long necks so elegant
They flicker their long eyelashes
And observe us triumphant
As they move with grace and beauty
Loping from one tree to the next

To eat leaves from highest branches
Which other animals may resent.

Elephants have passed here
The evidence remains
Broken trees and battered grasses
Leaving wide open lanes.
Looking closely we even see
Vegetable ivory undigested
Soft outer shells eaten
By elephants as they feasted.
One emerges near to us
Swinging its trunk from side to side
And now we are vulnerable
It's time to resume the ride.

So it's onwards to the waterhole
Before it is too hot
Here the animals will gather
And will be easier to spot.
We watch as antelopes sip carefully
And elephants lugubriously gather
Keeping the young between them
Jostled between father and mothers.
Legs splayed, the giraffes bend
And sink their long necks low
But all here are still anxious
They mustn't be too slow.

Predators must drink too
And are never far away
This is no time to relax

Nor the place to stay.
It's time for us to go now
And leave the animals to live
Give birth and nurture
Until surely they must die.
We'll take our memories with us
And our photos too
In the future we'll remember
This was an adventure not a zoo.

LINDEN SWEENEY
Little Neston

I have always written in many forms: everything from poetry to academic articles.
This group of writers has allowed me a place to explore my writing further. Over the last five years, I have learned so much from them. Our group is a safe and supportive space to be creative and to make strong friendships. I am sure readers of this anthology will see what a diverse range of styles and interests we have.

HOUSE SOUNDS

At night, the wind soughs in the pines
as the hard rain falls on the window
and the long Wrexham train rattles by.

At first light, a blackbird sings
though the rain still falls apace
and the gulls have flown in from the sea.

By day, the motors whirr
of washers and dryers and mowers
and, still, there is wind in the trees.

Above me, the magpies dance,
heavy footed, on the roof
and skeins of geese honk past.

Inside, there is the click of a kettle
and the tink of my ring on a cup
and the sounding of words in my head.

At evening tide, when quiet falls,
there is the soft settling of a log
and silence, sometimes.

THE DECORATED CITY

Blood red lanterns
swing like bodies
from the gibbets
 of skeletal trees;
the hanging remains
of Chinese New Year
abandoned,
redundant,
unwanted.

The gypsy trumpeter plays
'On the street where you live'
while the boy on the windy corner,
bearded, dirty and drugged
slips on a cardboard pillow,
at the level of passing dogs.

Bare legged girls with dirty knees
smoke cigarette butts
on Colquitt Street and Wood Street,
on Slater Street
and Seel.

The city is awash;
its doorways brimful,
the basement are as inundated,
overflowing into the gutters.
This is not a sudden high tide,
nor an unforeseen deluge.
It is a seepage of the unsettled,

a discharge of the disinherited,
an excretion of the exiled,
the drip, drip, drip of the houseless,
the abandoned,
the redundant,
the unwanted
decoration of the city.

FLAMENCO

The tambourine
Flutters its heartbeat
as the dancer turns her head,
looking behind to lock her gaze
on the eyes of the gypsy guitar
as he plucks out
the rhythm in her eyes.
She moves with him, her feet
feeling the ritual patterns,
drawn from deep within.
Her steps slow,
precise at first,
gathering intensity.
The tempo rises,
her shining black shoes
building into a blur
of wild flamenco stamping.
The castanets gleaming beetle-wings
hiss in her hand.
Red silk skirts sizzle,
flaming, lifted
in a sinuous figure of eight.
Then, like hot coals, dropped,
cooling to a swirling circle;
a scarlet puddle of blood around her feet.

With a toss of her crown and an arching of her back,
the dancer's arms become the handles of the chalice;
Her fingers, the final staccato ornaments.
Clicking again and pulsing
in communion with the rhythm of her body;
the offering circles in time to the strumming,
becomes the throbbing duende of the dance.

THE MAN I WAS ON THURSDAY

If I could just retrace my dusty steps,
each one stepping back behind the other,
my heavy pack might weigh me down,
my legs might feel so heavy,
but still, I would go back and back,
to the man I was,
on Thursday.

If I could place each foot there,
in each footprint in the sand,
I would not mind the heat and dust.
I would walk backwards
all the long, weary miles to base,
to the man I was,
on Thursday.

If I could only relive the day.
Just put my finger on rewind;
on fast replay
to breakfast time that day,
sitting down with all my mates,
being just the man I was,
on Thursday.

If I could press pause
and hold my foot mid-air,
I would stand on one-leg forever, like a fool.
I would not make that fatal footstep
on the unexploded, improvised device.
I would still be all the man I was,
on Thursday.

REMAINDER OF THE DAY

That time of year you may just see in me
when work is done, the harvest gathered in.
When wrinkled leaves are hanging from the trees
and winter's preparations now begin.
You think you see in me the evening shadows
of night's dark clouds that will obscure the sun,
the summer warmth now with cold opposed
and only night's dark promise yet to come.
But you are wrong to see me in this light.
The remainder of my day is still to come
with still time to accomplish all I might.
My time's my own, a new life's just begun.
You may see me now as old and grey.
You are wrong: this is the best part of the day.

(Based on Shakespeares's Sonnet 73 *with a nod to Kazuo Ishiguro's* Remains of the Day.*)*

BETH TAYLOR
Parkgate

I was given a book mark recently picked up at a Children's book fair. The tag line, which I just love is 'why try to fit in when you were born to stand out'. Such a positive message for young readers and writers of all ages. I am more of an avid reader than a writer but was persuaded to join the Group by a dear friend. I have so enjoyed the time spent with this very talented group of writers and have learned so much. I am constantly in awe of their work.

WHEN AUTUMN LEAVES START TO FALL

I remember, can you remember when
Was it that summer, no it was autumn
We were awed by the spectacle of the leaves
Each tree different, some at the end most at the start
The colour changes from green to red to gold to
How can I describe the splendour of the fall?

(Inspired by this song composed by Joseph Kosma with lyrics by Jacques Prévert and performed most famously by Nat King Cole.)

MAKING WAVES vs COMMON GROUND

Malicious, malevolent masterful manipulation of words
Acrimony abounds
Keep trotting out same old same old
Inflicting blows and causing pain
Nothing new, nothing constructive
Going round and round in circles
Why do we do this to ourselves
Always them and us and never we
Very destructive, very wearing
Every battle is a war
Something needs to change

Cease fire required right now
Olive branches needed
Maybe hatchets need to be buried
More listening than talking would be good
Offer support not demolition
Nurture good ideas with good grace
Give credit where it's due
Respect others' right to hold a different opinion
Observe body language, build on consensus
Understand your own prejudices and limitations
Never give up looking for common ground
Don't make waves

I COME FROM

I come from the windswept north east of Scotland
Cold and bleak in winter
And sometimes in summer too
Our City, famed for Jute, Jam and Journalism

I come from a Mother who was 1 of 14 children
But could only remember 6 others
She worked in Jute Mills with her 2 sisters from the age of 13
She was a weaver and loved it – she loved all her many jobs

I come from a large extended family
It seemed like a cast of thousands to my younger self
So many cousins, whose children were whose
Simple pleasures, not much money but happy times

I come from a Father born of Highland country folks
His Father, the Engineer in Knockando Distillery – renamed Cardhu
He worked there briefly but was destined to be a railwayman
A train driver, every small boy's dream, a good man, a good Dad

MARRIAGE SECOND TIME AROUND

Thoughts of the Bride as she walks down the aisle
The expectations are overwhelming
Exhaustion has set in
All the planning, the deliberations
Who to please, who to disappoint
The expense, the stress, will it be worth it?
Am I doing the right thing?
Is it too late to change my mind?
Too late the die is cast
He may not be the most dynamic
He may not be the love of my life
He is kind, a good person
He is a safe pair of hands

Thoughts of the Groom as he awaits his Bride
OMG am I doing it again?
I vowed I wouldn't but here goes
I can tell she'll be good for me
She loves my Son and he likes her
Nothing can go wrong this time
I'll make sure of that I promise
The music fills the church
Here comes the Bride

(Inspired by an old wedding photograph album, circa 1960.)

MY HELICOPTER RIDE FROM ANTIGUA TO MONTSERRAT

The pilot, a very nice young Canadian, gave us lots of data about the island. A British protectorate measuring 10 x 8 kilometres which used to have approx 11000 residents before the first volcanic eruption and was now around 1200 after the third eruption in 1995. One third of the south, including the capital Plymouth, had been designated off limits as the volcano was still very much active.

Our pilot first took us round the northern area which was so lush and green then headed out to sea to approach the island from the south. He explained that the flow was measured as moving at 100 mph and the rock shelf created in the sea and clearly visible from above had taken 3 minutes to travel from the volcano to the shore obliterating everything in its path.

We flew over what had been the capital town of Plymouth, everything was grey, no vegetation to be seen as far as the eye could see. Clearly visible in the middle of this lunar-like landscape was a church spire totally intact and it took a few seconds to register that the church, and indeed every other building in what had been a thriving town, was buried beneath thousands of tons of ash which had rained down.

The only other recognisable sign of what had been before was the iconic blue logo of Barclays Bank. A giant cylinder lay on its side and our Pilot confirmed that this was a gas storage tank which had been 3 miles from town before the eruption.

Beyond Plymouth there were few properties which stood untouched, like islands in this unworldly wilderness. One still had its picket fence and gate with a few shrubs on either side, standing like an oasis in a grey desert. As we flew on, miraculously we witnessed a few cows and sheep managing to survive on the slim pickings available to them.

It was an overwhelming experience to see at first hand the devastation wreaked by the power of nature and it continues to be the most profound experience of my life.

MARY WHITE
Neston

I love being part of Neston Writers held in the community centre every two weeks. A prompt is given in turn by a member which produces the most amazing short stories and poems. I find it an excellent way of keeping the brain cells working.

DOOR KEY

She rang the bell, there was no answer but at least they had left the key in the lock, they had known she was calling.

The door opened to her turn and she entered the dreary narrow hall and called 'Mr. Jones, I'm here.' She waited but no one answered. How many times since she had started her new round had she visited identical housing estates when you were left to find what you needed on your own.

Oh well must get on, she thought, exasperated, they call you out then aren't ready when you get here. She peeped into the front room then the back but there was no sign of life.

She called again; nothing!

Oh well, I haven't got all day so she ascended the stairs to the dark landing and called 'Mr Jones.'

She listened and from the front bedroom she heard the snores of someone in a deep sleep. So there he was tucked up, out for the count, oblivious to her presence under a heap of duvet, only his baldhead visible on a grubby pillow. She hung her coat on the landing and set about getting her equipment ready and pulling an apron and gloves from her bag.

Making as much noise as possible she rummaged about for a bowl and ran the tap till it was full of hot water. She placed the pouch in the warmth and tramped into the bedroom once more, not a movement evident from the supine figure.

'Mr. Jones,' she called, her tone an octave louder, feeling annoyed and impatient, but this was followed by anxiety. Was he ok? Back in the bathroom she gathered some towels and the bowl with the pouch and tramped once more into the sleeper's room. She laid them on the dressing table and approached the bed.

'Mr Jones,' she called, lifting the duvet gently. The eyelids blinked open. A look of horror crossed his face. He shot into sitting position, pulling the duvet under his chin.

'Who the hell are you?'

'Mr, Jones, I'm sorry to wake you, I've called to give you your enema.'

'Not bloody likely you are. Who let you in?'

'You left the key in the door for me. I'm your new nurse; your enema is due today.'

'I left the key in the door for my neighbour to drop in some milk.'

'You are Mr. William Jones, aren't you?'

'No luv, I'm John Barnes and I've been on night shift in Cadburys, now you've woken me and I won't be able to get back to sleep!' he barked.

Shamefaced she made her apologetic exit scolding herself for not checking the road signs more carefully; Dale Crescent was identical to Dale Way.

AFTER MASS

What I would give to walk with you in the graveyard
After Sunday Mass listening to you recite the history
On the grey lichened crosses and headstones;
Constance, married a town solicitor and cut off by her family
Not for religious reasons as was presumed
But because he was not top drawer, titled like them.
The infant set alight playing with matches in his cot,
The woman put away after childbirth and left in the asylum.

I'd yawn; 'You've told me that before,' I'd quip bored;
The smart Alec reaction of the young.
Unheeding on you spoke in your soft lilt,
Your eyes a diamond blue as the distant Mournes;
Robin, the lone Protestant adrift from his family burial ground,
The shell-shocked soldier no one understood.   All interred
To face the rising sun.   How I would listen to your narrative
If I could walk once more with you through the narrow aisles
On that hallowed ground of a townland chapel.

Now the gap between us is a deep chasm, for you
Like the departed whose sad histories you recalled
Are a chiselled name like all the dead on a headstone too.

BAPTISMAL PARTING

It was a ritual function of his farewell parting,
To guard and guide us for a new task or strange destination.
As a child I felt safe with each Baptism,
Believing I could act in the school play,
Or travel anywhere alone, shielded by his blessing.
Then as a teenager with back-combed hair,
I scolded, rolled my eyes and sneered.
It was the urgent item bottled in the kitchen press,
Brought home from pilgrimages or drawn from Ladywell on the 15th.
There is no filled font now inside the door,
No pious hand to cast with his mystic mist
The safety-netted halo that once surrounded me,
But I see him still, my father determined with each parting
Despite my cynic smile to bless me into the future years!

MAGIC

Oh yes, just the thing, Mavis thought as she admired the reflection in the full-length mirror in her bedroom. Her mid calf dress in rich dark green velvet was as smooth as an avocado and she caressed the flat surface of her stomach repeatedly. The promised satisfaction was gratifying and she had to admit, though disliking that pair Trinny and Susannah, they were correct about Magic knickers.

It had been such a struggle dragging them on and her face was now flushed and sweaty but it was worth it when she surveyed the results. She hadn't been quite honest about the size but she could squeeze into a medium just for tonight. The high waist stopped a muffin top and the mid thigh masked all that ugly cellulite. *Lifts and Supports* it said on the package she tore open excitedly. *70 Denier to smooth out and prevent overhang*.

The restaurant he took her to was dark and romantic, music soft and soothing drifted from a raised platform where the pianist in evening dress gently tapped the keys. The waiter pulled out the chair, flicked a large linen napkin on her lap then lit a red candle twined with budding roses. Ian sampled the wine, approved and they drank to good times.

A light starter was best, the salmon mousse and she nibbled daintily as he tucked into thick vegetable soup and chunks of French crusty bread. The chicken in rich sauce was filling but she couldn't resist the asparagus and buttered new potatoes. She declined dessert as the waist constriction was beginning to object to eating more and she thought she had been a tad foolish to have bought the medium.

'I insist,' Ian smiled encouragingly, 'Go on spoil yourself. After all it's a special occasion, us meeting was the best thing that's happened to me.'

The fudge cake, smothered in a Bailey's cream was his favourite, she must have some! Her polite refusal was over-ruled. Now she was struggling and she thought of Victorian ladies laced into tight corsets to maintain their hourglass figures. No wonder they fainted a lot, for her tight hosiery was strangling her as their wasp waists must have strangled them.

'You must try the wonderful local cheeses.' The strong aroma produced a wave of nausea.

God I'm going to be sick, she thought as she hurriedly excused herself before she made a disgusting exhibition of herself on their first evening out together.

Bending over in the ladies was excruciating. A splash of cold water calmed her burning face and surveying herself in the mirror was horrified at flushed skin and panda eyes, black trickles smudged her puffy cheeks. She fumbled in the depths of her handbag. Thank God, they were there!

She returned to the cubicle and began hacking at the expensive undergarment with her tiny nail scissors. It took almost ten minutes to decimate the bloody masochistic thing but the joy, the relief when she bundled it into the bin.

He looked disapprovingly at the dishevelled bulky woman. 'You've been a long time so I've had my coffee,' he declared, 'perhaps we should go now.'

A SIXTIES MEMORY

The young women stood at the top of the wide staircase hesitantly. The building being mid Victorian had no lift. Slowly they began their descent. Pale as a ghost the red-head carried a small case while the other in uniform gripped the heavy banister as a support tightly gripping the bundle in her arm's crook, her fingers open wide as a starfish. Neither spoke as they trod each polished stair. A soft sob followed the sniffles as they quickly glanced in each other's eyes.

    Nurse Green could think of no comforting words. She had never done this before and her mind felt too confused to match the thoughts her heart felt. Kathy's red curls fell halfway across her blotchy cheek. It had all been so exciting last summer moving to Liverpool to start her first year at the teacher training college, a place of such liveliness compared to her home in the Lake District. Her parents were so proud of her but not anymore, that dream was shattered to smithereens. As strict Catholics they were horrified.

    The frumpy woman waiting in the hall below looked up without a word of greeting. She opened the heavy door and propped it with her foot like a wedge.

    'I'll take him now, nurse, just hold this open please.'

    Nurse Green ladled the bundle into her arms and watched as the driver of the white taxi opened the door and the woman spooned herself and the baby onto the back seat and drove towards the hospital exit without another word.

    'Good luck Kathy,' was all she could say as she watched the weeping figure walk away to the future.

JENNY WILLIAMS
Port Sunlight Village

Forty years have passed between my first dalliance with writing poetry, and my second. So much more life to draw upon these days. Hopefully my selection will illustrate that I can't predict what inspires me.

BOLERO

Swaying
Kneeling iris ombre figures
Nearly touch, so compelling
Glinting blades not yet propelling
Slowly, smoothly, music swelling.

More bars
Figures rise, blades engage
Dancers destiny unfolding
Forty million eyes upholding
The pace is rolling rolling rolling.

Partners
Show artistic interpretation
Synchronicity on the ice
Result of dogged practice
But is the romance artifice?

Building
How will the play conclude?
This tragic Romeo and Juliet.
The dancers love – and yet and yet,
Prostrate, the bodies and the ice have met

FREE YOUR MIND

File away the people pleaser
Retire the hesitancy
Ease out the worries
Erase the painful memories.

You can still care, and
Operate with empathy, but
Understand your own needs
Respect *your mind and body*

Make time to live
Invite contentment to invade
Never doubt yourself
Dare to dream.

NEW YEAR'S EVE

A half moon in a blue grey sky
Gives an optimistic wink
On New Year's Eve.
Some competition for the smouldering sun
Lazy in its showing late today.

A grid shape forms in white
From all those planes so recently rare
Making haste to unlocked destinations
Returning from far flung isles
Human additions to the firmament.

The new year yields snow
A delicate icing sugar dusting
Lingering where feet don't tread
Where tyres don't grind
Where boughs hold out sanctuary.

Catch a snowflake in your palm
Marvel at water spun like a web
Forming its unique pattern
But right at the door of extinction
From the gift of your heat.

WALKING THE LABYRINTH

What if this road was walked with good company
comfortable shoes, fine weather?
Not as a twisted,lonely,painful, barefoot
trek, such as it has become?
A camino of the lost soul.

There would be snack shacks, vistas,
Memories made, a dearth of traffic.
But contorted, I cannot easily put one foot
In front of the other.
Progress, a chain of jerky movements.

I speak to the birds , and the sun.
I have no friends to lean upon.
I throw my head back, and holler at the sky.
Raindrops fall and catch the tongue, stuck out
In a moment of rebellion.

Replenished, I meet a fellow
traveller on life's pathway, who smiles.
We are heading in the same direction it seems,
I find I have a companion on this
convoluted curve.

ACKNOWLEDGEMENTS

After years of meeting in person, it is a delight to see our work published in an anthology! There are a number of people without whom this wouldn't have been possible.

Firstly we want to thank all of our writers who contributed to this - Maureen, Margaret, Ishbel, Debbie, Pauline, Jean, Chris, Linden, Beth, Mary and Jenny. Your creative contribution to this anthology is much appreciated.

We want to give special thanks to our members who put extra time and effort into getting this publishing. Thank you Beth and Margaret for editing and collating everyone's work.

Thank you as well to Margaret's daughter Lydia for publishing this and designing the front cover.

Finally, thank you to YOU for reading this! As writers, it means everything to have our poetry and short stories read!

Printed in Great Britain
by Amazon